What a Catastrophe!

by Wayne Campbell

Pictures by Eileen Christelow

BRADBURY PRESS/NEW YORK

The text originally appeared in
What a Catastrophe!
published in Australia
by Ashton Scholastic

Bradbury Press
An Affiliate of Macmillan, Inc.
866 Third Avenue, New York, NY 10022
Collier Macmillan Canada, Inc.
Printed and bound in Japan
10   9   8   7   6   5   4   3   2   1

The text of this book is set in Clearface
The illustrations are pen and ink, colored pencils, and
water color
Book design by Lynn Braswell

Library of Congress Cataloging-in-Publication Data

Campbell, Wayne.
What a catastrophe!

Summary: A young boy relates what happens when he
brings a frog home for breakfast. The reader is invited
to choose the ending.
1. Plot-your-own stories.   [1. Frogs—Fiction.
2. Humorous stories.   3. Plot-your-own stories]
I. Christelow, Eileen, ill.   II. Title.
PZ7.C1612Wh   1986   [E]   86-18871
ISBN 0-02-716420-9

I don't know what it's like at your place,
but at my house, when I get up,
nobody else is even out of bed.

This morning, it was just the same,
so I went for a walk.

It was meant to be a short walk.
But I ended up going down the road,
around the corner, and through the fence . . .

Then I saw
something sitting in the long grass.

It was this **BIG!**

No—it was really only
this big.

It was green.
It was a green-spotted something.
It was a green-spotted frog.

I said, "Good morning, Frog,
and how do you do?"
The green-spotted frog said, "Croak!"
I said, "Let's go home for breakfast."
The green-spotted frog said, croak!"

I picked it up, put it in my pocket,
and went home.

I got there just in time.
Mom yelled, "Breakfast's ready!"
Dad yelled, "Now!"

So I sat down at the table and completely
forgot about the frog in my pocket.

I soon found out that the frog
did not want to be forgotten.
It hopped out of my pocket
and onto my lap.
But it didn't stop there...

It hopped onto the table.
But it didn't stop there, either.

It hopped along the table and landed, **PLOP**, right in a bowl of cereal.

The green-spotted, cereal-coated frog
kept jumping and jumping and making a terrible mess.

My father, who can get very grumpy and angry,
looked very grumpy and angry!

My mother, who loathes creepy-crawlies
and nasty-bities and green-spotted,
cereal-coated, mess-making frogs,
really looked alarmed.

My brother, who loves cereal, just sighed

and kept spooning it in.

My sister, who's always as quiet as a mouse,
just giggled and giggled. She must have
known that there was going to be trouble.

My baby brother, who can't walk or talk
yet, isn't scared of anything. He looked
at the green-spotted, cereal-coated,
mess-making frog jumping up and down,
and thought it was just great.
He opened his arms and tried to catch it.

I didn't know whether to laugh or cry.
I didn't know whether to run or hide.
So I put my hands right over my eyes
and tried, really tried, not to laugh.

It was a catastrophe. A real disaster.

But what about the frog? What about
the green-spotted, cereal-coated,
mess-making, catastrophe-causing frog?
What could have happened to it?

ENDING 1

It was only a frog. A dear, old, harmless,
green-spotted frog that I brought home.
Only one.
But I was banned from bringing home anything.
ANYTHING!
No more worms, snails, caterpillars,
stray dogs, slugs, slimies, cockroaches,
crickets, snakes, mice, tadpoles, ferrets,
sick birds, one-eyed cats, or frogs!
They wouldn't change their minds
even though I caught the frog
and put it back where I found it.

ENDING 2

My baby brother, who can't catch very well,
did catch the green-spotted, cereal-coated,
mess-making, catastrophe-causing frog.
He squeezed the slippery, slimy frog
so tightly that it shot up
and **bounced**
off the ceiling.
The last time I looked I could still
see the cereal mark.

ENDING 3

My sister, who just giggled and giggled,
picked up the frog
and gave it a big **kiss**.

And, of course, it turned
into a handsome prince.

My father, who can get very grumpy
and angry, swiped at the

green-spotted, cereal-coated, mess-making,
catastrophe-causing frog.

It flew across the room, jumped out
of the window, and hopped down
the road, around the corner,
through the fence, back to the
safety of the long green grass.